LOVE LIKE YOU

JANNET RF

Made with ♥ on the Notion Press Platform
www.notionpress.com

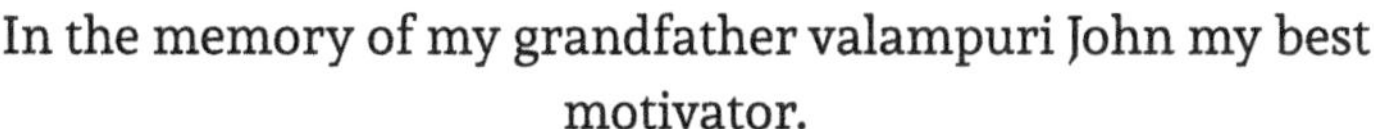

In the memory of my grandfather valampuri John my best motivator.

dedicated to my beloveds who inspired Me in everything.

dedicated to my heavenly Father Jesus who is and was always there for me.

Thank you for your love and Compassion throughout these year's.

Contents

FOREWORD

Look for more inspirational series@amazon.com/ flipkart.com/notionpress.com and aslso

available in Kindle

NOVELS

Summer love the one i cherish

The tournamnet

Love like you

Saturdays are always special

Reality love

New begining

Its always you

CHILDRENS BOOKS

#Short stories

The tales of the magical kingdom

COLORING BOOKS

Princess coloring book

Floral art

DEVOTIONAL BOOK

Mother mary biography

St. anthony biography

Preface

Love like you novel tells about the confusion that goes undeer each and every person

and each and every person loves Rose more than anything

finally they come into a conclusion that only Sam can pursue Rose and understand her

as Rose and her friends participates in the music program which decides their future

they intentionally upload a music video on hteir own and somehow it got super popular

One day Rose meet's Daniel and he call's her gorlfriend infront of everyone and Sam who watches

the news gets's mad and warns him to stay away from him

As college ends everyone goes on their carrier path were they only get time to meet on Saturday

Also 2 version of books available in amazon.com/flipkart.com/notionpress.com alsp available in kindle.

#Summer love the one i cherish

#The tournament

Acknowledgements

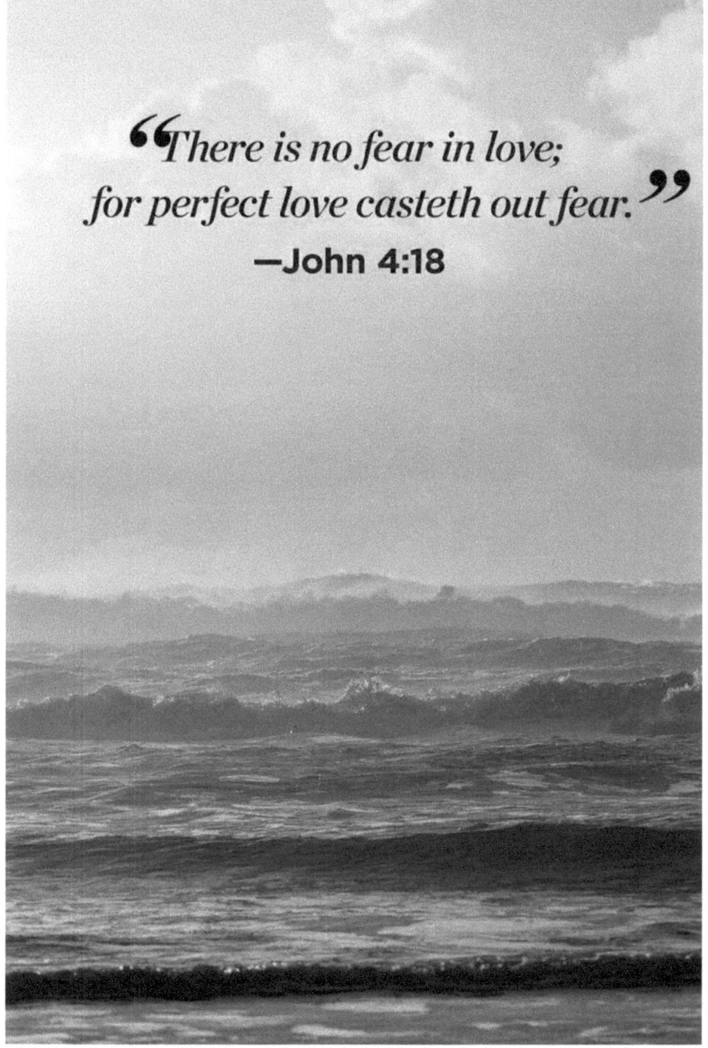

Prologue

LOVE LIKE
YOU
JANNET RF

I

THE COMPETITION

This is real ,this is me , this is where I'm supposed to be, na na na ... na na yup I think this should do the trick . what trick ? asked John as he entered the basement with snacks on his hands , "it was a beautiful sunny day and early spring to start a fresh new start" , "i was preparing for a music competition , oh really ! asked John excited so that's why you wanted my basement he laughed out so loud , i nearly thought it was something more elite ,"and just what are you thinking asked Rose with a scornful look on her face" : hey no need to get all worked up about , i was just kidding ,"you better be entered a male voice breaking their conversation" , Kevin ! said John forcing a smile on his face that he almost wanted to kick him in his ass.

Rose didn't mind those two and she started eating the snacks John bought inside the basement , she wanted to avoid her headache so she didn't mind them at all "Kevin who invited you here anyway , smacked John on gis back , oh i just thought leaving you two alone won't do any good for me , oh ! so your saying that your in love with Rose ? "I've always loved her besides i just want her to be happy " Sam entered their conversation when John was staring at Kevin still his hands on his shoulder , "oh look at you two , making love , that's cute , "Rose almost threw up hearing what Sam just said now , she laughed continuously that she couldn't stop .. you guy's hahaha stop it ,my tummy hurts , "Sam was happy to see her laugh so did John and Kevin , hey dude what are you , making pass at me ? asked Kevin ,

John blushed furiously and he pushed Kevin with both his hands saying knock it off Kevin . "who knows maybe John will fall for Kevin soon , don't you think Rose ? " yeah she laughed , John urged in and told common Rose , it's just a misunderstanding , and the three of them nodded their heads unanimously smiling at John almost as agreeing as they can : do you think this song will do ? asked Rose beeaking the silence , the three of them turned towards her and asked her what song ? ,Rose gave a blunful expression saying i was asking John , but John was very silent for a moment and asked Rose that he wanted to talk to her in private with a serious look on his face " oh that's never gonna happen beemed up a voice , Rose thought oh god i hope it doesn't end in chaos "

"John turned to see who it was with an unpleasant look on his face but Sam urged and enclasped him saying alrighty , no need to get so worked up about , we are all friends , well except me thou but I think it's good to discuss frds thi ga to frds and not privately " so your saying that we should discuss anything together anything at all ? well not everything but most of it we can discuss it , i probably think it's not something private to talk about , John paused a second and looked at Sam saying you can talk whatever you want can't you ? You just want to know everything what i and Rose discuss , how pathetic are you Sam the famous basketball player and he left the place without a word "um does anyone knows that it's his home and he is actually going out, John came fast as he walked out fast blushing furiously, Sam you big jerk , John you lunatic and they both started laughing "

On the other hand Rose and Kevin was totally blanked out , i guess we are all a big lunatic said Rose and everyone started laughing till they felt the abdominal pain . "It was 12 in the afternoon and Rose was going through her e-mail thoroughly to make sure that she doesn't want to miss the invitation that she received from the band called the Rock of edge , she felt very lucky to be selected" , tring tring rang her phone she ignored it for the first time but it ranged the second time when she actually tried to pin the mail and it disappeared , she attended the call in anger and started shouting John for god's sake why did you call me , my e - mail is gone , John wet blank and then he told her forget about the e-mail Rose I'm with the Rock of edge , come to the stadium and hurry , what ! Shouted Rose and John cut the call knowing that she will definitely come

Absolutely said Kevin to the Rock of edge band , So your good at drums ugh ? teased Sam , uff common it's not like you don't know how to play drums ? , well actually... "Hey shouuted Rose from 10 distance away , panting heavily she then began saying , you guy's ! What are you doing here ? You guy's she asked them with a smile .. um hey Rose said Sam looking at her confused because he was aware of one thing that she is going to get mad hearing thia news , " oh Rose hello said the lead singer of the Rock band , he told her that it's a pleasure to meet you , your team number is 11 well Rock the stage and good luck and he left really fast as thin air" and Rose whispered Team !? .. oh hi waved , John , Sam and Kevin ....what ? you guy's are my team , yeah thy said in chorus , "do you guy's know the song ? don't worry about it said John , we got it covered .

The crowd went wild when Rose started singing , it was that feeling she never had and she finally got it , despite of everything she never knew she would actually sing with her friends and that made her sing even louder and the whole night it was crazy and full of noise more than music . A music band called the crown were making jeers at Rose , John pinned the boy on the wall and warned him with an eye to eye scare , it made the boy run but Rose was not aware of anything she just asked John what happened ? he just smiled at her and said , oh it's nothing he had a bug on his shoulder so i pinned him in the wall , oh ! really ? it doesn't seem that convincing but I'll try to believe you , on the other end the team Rock band was going to announce the winner of the competition so they were

seated at their places , Rose heart was pounding really fast ,she was okay if she lost that is if her fang lost she just wished what if she dus win and it would be amazing , the winner was someone else's gang but they got the third place and they were so happy and now they can audition anywhere , they got their liscence but they need to get liscence for the world music group so they knew they hard to work hard , hey John she hi-fi with him and also with Sam and Kevin , the three boy's were so happy to see Rose in high spirits so they decided to pursue her till their last breath the rock band lead singer shaked hands with Rose , it made Sam , Kevin mad they really didn't like anyone touching even her hand , it made them go crazy as an drynkard but since the lead singer was the one who supported them they just backed off and silenced themselves

He could just shut up , what's all the embarlment about , his eye balls were circling all over Rose I'm going to kill him said John in a low voice , " you don't need to ,look there Rose is coming over smiling at you , John was happy but Sam took his moment and held Rose in his both hands and smiled at her , Rose blushed and was furious , i um. It's okay said Sam i won't let you go or let you off that easily" , hey shouuted a voice from Sam's back , it's not appropriate to hold her like this in front of us you big goof ! Sam laughed and said ,she is going to be my wife some day , what's the issue John ? John said you can do whatever you want alone , but not in front of us , okay okay , looks like someone is getting jealous What ! I'm not getting jealous said John but on the other hand Rose was still blushing and Kevin noticed that , looks like she began to fall for him again , i hope John can take it easy or maybe not i guess I should tell him soon before it's too late.

II

PLANS FOR COLLEGE

The early morning breeze made Rose body shiver as it was still early in the morning but she woke up and sat in her bed her hair all messed up but she still looked beautiful her lips a red as before , her cheeks rosy color ,

she began to recall everything what happened yesterday and it made her lips even brighter she fell on her bed softly as an flower "hey Rosy you look beautiful" ,

Rose turned around and saw Sam on the window she was shocked and paralyzed he just came in casually without making any noise ,

"hey beautiful looking hot , Rose was still paralyzed and finally she came back to her sense and said ugh ?" , Sam kissed her and said yesterday you were awesome so should we have some fun ? ,

what said Rose , i ..well thanks um i .. Sam saw how Rose hesitated to even speak clearly he kissed her again and said 8AM at our usual spot were we used to have breakfast ,

I'll see you there said Sam and he went smiling at her , Rose was still blushing and her heart was pounding really fast , that man ..ugh he is making me blush , i better get ready soon before he plans something else .

Do you seriously want to do this and especially why are you dragging us into it Sam , i'm not going to dance you hear me ! , "

oh ! well alright then Kevin and i will dance with Rose while you watch us dancing in agony" ,

what Rose is in our music video too ?

"duh !

so who is the goof ball now ?

"you are said John smacking his back ,

Kevin gave an eye contact to Sam that Rose has come ,

"Rosy come here said Sam waving his hand ,

John was depressed hearing the word Rosy ,

it's because he was the first and only person to call her like that and that made him absurd,

well probably he thought of leaving but he reminded himself that he has to do the music video with her ,

so he made plans on his own schedule that no one will interfere his secret plan for Rose ,

"hey guy's said Rose waving her hand when she saw Sam she remembered the kiss ,

well of course it was not her first kiss but it was her first on her pajama's and it was transparent suddenly the thought of it made her blush even furious ,

she stood up and said i need to use the loo ,

oh um alright said Sam but he did notice that she was blushing so hard that he could easily tell it was because of him ,

"okay spill it said John staring at him giving him a grimace look on Sam ,

Sam told him it's none of your business John he said it having a bite of his chicken burger ,

fine ! said John and he started eating his , Kevin barged int their stupid conversation and said excuse me guy's i'll be back in 5 ,

sure said John and Sam chorusely

besides it would have been great if he actually didn't come thought John and Sam on their heads ,

but Kevin went outside were Rose was sitting on a bench and taking deep breath ,

Rose was thinking that this shouldn't go on like this ,

i alway's feel un comfortable in front of him and she shouted with both her hands up saying I ain't gonna blush anymore ,

ain't gonna blush asked Kevin smiling at her ,

oops ! i mean haha .. well ..it's okay said Kevin i know everything you can be in ease , he is yours somehow ,so you don't have to worry ,

Rose smiled back and said you're right and they both went back inside they saw Sam and John discussing about the music video ,

"i heard from Kevin he said that you guy's plan to make a music video

" but i don't know what to sing , Sam said don't worry it's alright we've got it covered ,

oh really ! asked John making a face at Sam yes , really really , and he turned to Rose and Kevin and told them that they are going to sing the cover of back street boys ,"everybody" ,

"you gotta be kidding me said John and Kevin , Rose was excited to hear but then again she told them that we need to practice really good ,

Sam said yes okay 3 times and then we do the music video i've called my camera men and they are already present at my studio ",

"your studio ? asked John a little un comfortable , um Sam why bother let's go to my company were i specially gifted Rose for her birthday .

Yeah she knows , but she ain't seen my studio yet, so let's go and make the video instead of bugging in ..and get inside the car , .. seriously .. said Sam almost disgusted as ever by John knowing that they were just going to practice ,

jeez what's his problem , thought Sam while their way to the stadium.

It took 15 min and they reached the stadium which was really big and it had Rose name on the top of the building wall and her photo ,

it was a dream probably ,but it's still real , she only imagined and it made her so happy and so crazy that she began to cry so much she thanked Sam and she did remember that even John did the same for her ,

so she hugged them both ,because she didn't want John to feel insecure at any cost because she knew that it was always him who made things right for her and was always there for her when she was at her lowest ,she also pulled Kevin by her side .

This place is awesome said Rose , so did John "they clearly loved everything about the music studio and it was well designed ,Kevin took a one look at the building and said ,no wonder your dad is an brilliant architect ,no kidding said John and they all seated in one place and b egan to discuss about the music video,

"we do have to wear ab outfit for the music video right ? asked Rose" , the three of them nodded unanimously and they were ready to make the music video, it was hard at first but they somehow did it and finished their music video and Sam was editing it to make it look better .

Rose hurried to her sling bag to check who called her , it was her mom , she called her back Her mom totally abashed her , that she went speechless after talking for 10 min she hung up and came inside the room were Sam was almost over with editing the video but it was again John who noticed how vulnerable she looked , he ran to her and held

face , asking ,

"Rose what's wrong ,

what did your mother say ,

Rose was shocked to know how did he know it was her mom "

she began crying ,

she joined me in college and want's me to learn Arts

What ! said John ,

Sam nearly shouted and Kevin was speechless ,

but his wheels were turning on his head , saying that they can actually convince her mom to change her plan in joining Rose to the college John and Sam was so mad at her mom that they were shouting and breathing like dragons that couldn't control their anger ,

" Kevin urged in to their conversation to abate the situation

"Hey guy's why don't we calm down I know a way to convince her mom said Kevin ,

"Rose heart calmed down and she asked him still tears rolling in her eye balls ,, really !

"yes really "

he smiled back at her and he took a handkerchief he had in his shirt pocket and gave it to her , "here take this as a token of my gratitude , and everybody started laughing loud "when you guy's are here I don't think i have to be afraid of anything ,

the 3 of them blushed furiously seeing her smiling eye's

"what's taking this girl so long , i thought i told her to come in 5min , relax said Rose dad , you always gave her a hard time she is growing up ,

stop controlling her but she was abberant and Rose's father knew that she was jealous of her daughter.

Ahh ! there you are ? said Rose father looking at Rose ,

" well how was your day ?

he asked very polite and smiled at her passionately

" it was great dad i loved it

"well then what are your interest's in music my dear ?,

maybe you can pursue your dream by studying more about music"

for a moment Kevin was stunned ,

he didn't expect to undergo this sudden change ,but he was delighted to knew that something had to change ,and it was easy as a piece of cake ,

"her mother was mad like hell and started quarrelling with her dad , and she said awful things about Rose , that's when her dad gave her one tight slap and warned her

"if you ever ,speak ill of my daughter then be prepared to get a divorce from me " he told to Rose to take her friends to were they were hanging out recently ,

so they headed straight to the stadium .

"Okay we will go through which college we should all go said John resting his hand on the backseat of the car "

"i think you don't have to go through all those trouble John said Rose, what are you talking about i would do anything for you my princess

" Rose laughed and said okay my prince " i am serious Rose i would do anything for you , i know you would "

"Kevin urged in the conversation , i hate to break it to you , but your dad has already decided which college we all should go

" what ! exclaimed

Sam ,

John and Rose "I'm happy that we are all together in college too , and i think i should be grateful to you guy's,smiled Rose .

"Kevin , Sam and John said ,

no actually we should thank you to be in our lives You make us perfect"

"Rose smiled back at them and said well Music college , here we go ..yeah woooo"

"John asked Kevin exactly which college ?

oh ! St.Mathews replied Kevin smiling in the thoughts of happiness ,

but when he saw John's face , what's wrong ? "

"well that's were , Sarah and Leah goes to college" i checked the attendance record just now ,

you gotta be kidding me said Sam , nope I'm serious

"well then it's gonna be one hell of a year said Kevin "

" to st. Matthews then ,

no said John in a blunt voice , it's actually like going back to the past ".

III

NEW EVERYTHING

"Are you absolutely sure , that they go here ?"

I'm positive Said John to Kevin ,

well it's not like they are actually going to see us on the way

" a counteractive question said Rose as she pointed her fore finger to the left side of the building ,were Sarah and Leah was actually staring at them ,

when they noticed that all of them took a one look at them , they actually wanted to turn around and look where else but unfortunately they couldn't , so Sarah and Leah marched in front of them and Sarah said hey Rose how are you doing? ,

Rose was blank for a moment , but she went with the flow , i am doing great thanks Sarah , how have you been ? Sarah couldn't talk anymore , she began to cry so loud and said that she was sorry for everything she told about Rose , she really didn't had a good time without Rose ,and besides Rose was the first person who actually accepted her as a friend and always made her smile and even helped her with her dream , so she cried about how awful she behaved at Rose lately ,

" it's alright Sarah you don't need to worry about it , besides friends are always there for each other no matter what , smiled Rose looking at Sarah "

" Leah on the contrary wanted to submit her details as well for being mean to Rose without even knowing about her but rose intruded and said it's alright Leah you are our friend too , so no need to get yourself worked up about "

" by the way ,why you guy's joined in music college ? asked Sam , oh Leah is really good at music and i can sing , but that was not the real reason ,so .... "Hey shouuted a male from far off , it was the Rock band leader and Rose was the only one who was happy to see him while other's felt disgusted

to seem him , because everyone knew that the Rock band leader was eventually falling for her , and it was not like Rose was the only one who looked stunning " there were lots of girls who looked really good but they all knew that Rose had this one kind of charm that no one could possess and everyone was bound for it and none could ever escape from her charm or her kindness , it just seemed regardlessly impossible to escape.

So Rose you look really lovely today I hope we could collaborate with each other and make this unforgettable experience of the music college ,

" it's only for a year beemed up a voice ,

it was John , he just couldn't just keep his temper inside of him anymore " oh , but still isn't it lovely to collect beautiful memories , asked the Rock band leader , John knew that he couldn't keep up

he really didn't want the Rock band leader to pursue Rose or even look at her , and when the Rock band leader came close to Rose , suddenly a voice beemed up it was deep , it was none another then Kevin ,

"common Josh it's not nice to play with my girlfriend as he said he carried with his hands and she grabbed Kevin tight as it was a sudden move ,

everyone was awwed Sam was really irritated but at that moment if Kevin didn't make a move , then the Rock band leader wouldn't have stopped flirting with Rose and she was more naive enough to Realize it , but after Josh the Rock band leader left ,

Sam wanted to go after Rose but Sarah stopped him and said , Sam i think you should leave those two alone , why ! shouted Sam in rage anger ,

Sarah was startled that tears fell from her eye balls and Sam felt like a jerk for yelling at her and taking his anger on her seemed very ridiculous to him , "nice going basketball captain said Leah as she gave him a Scornful look for making her cry.

" Rose was staring at Kevin for carrying her In front of everyone especially her friends it was really embarrassing,

Kevin why did you carry me all the way here to the library ground ? ,

Oh I'm really sorry, Josh was making a move at you so i was really irritated so i carried you and .... and what said Rose looking at Kevin still blushing at him ,

what's wrong he asked Rose looking close to her face giving an eye contact, Rose was still blushing , and Kevin leaned to her lips and kissed her holding her body tight andhe couldn't control himself so he went all the way down to her neck ,but Rose didn't resist",

it semmed like she was okay with it he started to undo her shirt buttons but Rose pushed him away saying this is not a bedroom Kevin , oh ! so your okay if it's a bedroom ? teased Kevin smiling at her looking at her whole body of how precious

She was and winning her was like winning the whole world so Kevin thought of pursuing her no matter what , as he was on his own precious memories ,

Rose joggled all up pulling his hand saying let's go back

" wait a sec , what is it ? Do . .. you ..do you want to be my girlfriend?

a mysterious question and yet very decieving...Rose froze she suddenly pulled Kevin and kissed him and said i do want to be but let's keep it low key... Kevin said it would make things worse, let's tell our friends before it's too late,

then what about Sam ? asked Rose a little sad Kevin told Rose you don't have to force yourself to love me , let's talk this out so that no one get's hurt " okay but i wish no one really get's hurt!.

Jeez were did they go wined John with the guitar in his hand , he was really exhausted as he had to play the part of Kevin and Rose as they were not present at the moment

I'm going to kill him shouted John ! Sam was also in a bad mood as well but he kept quiet and didn't want to let his emotions out like John did ,

it's just it was not his type of expressing his feelings like a mirror in a direct way,

uff! finally Rose were did you go ? We have to practice remember?

I'm sorry John she said with a sad face ,

okay okay but no more going anywhere in the middle of restroom except for break time , got it said Rose,

okay let's start our practice 1,2,3 ..go .. After the practice Rose called Sam and said hey um .. it's alright he urged i don't see you that way Rose and I'm not going to force you to love me either way but i just ... John barged inside the conversation and said wait not so fast Sam you can't just say you don't have feelings for her ,

we all clearly know that you love Rose .."yes you all know but I need a brea from all of this mess I'm sorry Rose but I need to fulfill my needs first

I know my dad's a business man and filthy rich but i juyneed to make things right for myself and i know you can't wait.." I will wait shouted Rose with tears in her eyes , Sam couldn't control himself he cried too hugging her tight and said i know,

i know you would wait but it's gonna be okay this time you have everyone to take care of you , i will be back in a year " but why ? asked Rose ,

Sam said it's not my decision it's your father's , Rose was shocked but she didn't mind as long it's not his own decision she was okay with it Sam said look Rose it's alright even if you can't wait it's alright with me , I'm just saying incase you ought to change your mind it's okay with me , Rose didn't say much she told him let's just believe in fate .

John hurried to the car to stop Rose because he knew that she was not feeling good ,

"Hey Rosy wait up let me accompany you , Rose turned to see John who was already infront of her she hugged him tight and cried , it's alright let's get inside the car "

"Hey Kevin so planning to pursue Rose,

none of your business ,

hey common man you just admitted that she is your girlfriend ,

Kevin got fierce all of a sudden and pin pointed him at the wall and yelled stay out of my sight , the least you can do right now

" Kevin's mood was not good when he underwent the same situation exactly like last year except that this time he was actually in the situation and seeing John accompanying Rose made his mood even worse, as he was filled with undelighted things in his head , something made him happy when ge entered his room .

Sarah was already over with Sam's cranky attitude , she started cleaning her wardrobe which was full of clothes and makeup stuff ,

while she was cleaning she saw the first made dress while she was working with Rose all those memories made her smile and it made her clean the wardrobe even slower and it took till 5PM to finish all those shelves ,

man I'm warned out i should probably head out , maybe I'll call Leah too , yup that would be great.

IV

NEW FEELINGS

"Rose ! what are you doing here ?"

"what happened is something wrong ?"

"Rose smiled very silent with tears in her eyes , Kevin carried her and asked her to have a bath in the hot tub , but she didn't let him go she held his hand and asked him to give her the bath ,he was silent at first and then he continued "

what about Sam ? I'm through him said Rose , he looked at her very silent without making any noise , i remember everything ,when i was in coma you were the only one who was beside me you treated me like your wife , we actually got married and after that i don't know what happened but i want you to be with me forever that's all I want

Kevin cried and hugged her saying , promise me that you will never drift away can you promise me that ? " Yes i can promise you that i will be yours only forever",

he started removing her clothes gently at first Rose blushed as If a red paint was on her face ,

then he kissed her passionately and started to soap her and after finishing the bath he moaped her with the towel and gave her a comfortable dress to wear to get some sleep ,

" i .will go get you something to eat is chocolate okay ?

Mmm yeah she smiled at him ,

as Kevin left by Rose started to remove her clothes and she covered herself under the bed , when he came in she asked him let's intercourse with each other,i want it to be real and serious ,

Kevin was flustered then again he couldn't help it .. he did what she asked and very intense that made her body pain so bad that he took her to the bath again and this time he couldn't control his feelings and he fucked her up again,

she was moaning so bad that she shouted ...stop ..! Kevin .. ahhh .. "yes moan ahhh i want to hear you moan so loud. say my name Rose, say it. Ke...Kevin ahh ... and after a while Rose was resting in the bed and she was very tired ,

Kevin. held her by his side and rested his head on her breasts ... he just couldn't believe what was happening now was actually real .

"Leah was taking a bite of the fresh chocolate cake while Sarah was discussing about Rose and how they spent their time together ,

suddenly Leah's phone rang Oh my gosh ! What what's up ? ... Sarah you've been selected for the company at Los Angeles i mean you won the contest and your gonna work , wowww girl you rock ! , yup i sure do don't i , and they both laughed .

John was thinking deep and was out of blue thinking what was Rose was thinking he was not sure now because he was really confused on the thought of why she would ask him to stop to the near by shop and it was a coffee shop, " she only liked tea , but why?

...he paused for a moment as he was whispering in his own thoughts ...no ..no...she went to Kevin's home , but why

? "

Leah and Sarah were drifting like bubbles in the air hard to catch ,

" so looks like someone will be gone for a while now patted Leah on Sarah's shoulder very gently " aren't you coming with me? .. um ..well i already have a lot to take care of here and my dad wants me to check on every listing details of the company ,

he is actually training me so that i should not get fooled by other business people and moreover business can separate anything so i suggest you to follow your dreams my sweet Sarah , i mean after all this is what you have been fighting for a long

time so don't let this opportunity go to wastebe the here you wanna be ,be an example for your sister's smile Leah passionately ,

"but Sarah was thinking deep about something ,she didn't show it off she simply smiled back at her? well theb see ya gotta get back to home " we'll hold a party , what do you say? " " it's your wish since it's your last day at new York , i guess you should ".

" Sarah honey congratulation's on winning the competition ,i'm so proud of you hugger her mom " , well yes of course she is my daughter of course she will win said her father , but Sarah seemed blunt "i'll just head to my room guy's i feel a little tired , yeah honey okay have some rest "

should i call John ? well let me get some rest for now he is not my first priority so let me put this through and drown myself in deep sleep

A DREAM LAND

"John i love you " what? , "i said i'm in love with you " really , i love you too , Sarah i've been in love with you ever since i saw you in that shop when you came to by the

material's you want to buy ," but i thought you were in love with Rose ? , no i thought too but then i realized that i loved you more, after the fight we had , i just realized that it was you who made me think too much about you and i still can't stop thinking about you , so im gonna come and ask like a man , "Sarah samules will you love me and cherish me till the end and marry me for life

"what "!

oh my gosh it was just a dream , but why it's like this uff! i better take my mind of from these things and start planning for party decorations , as Sarah went down stairs after freshening herself up she saw John with a present in his hand , "oh Sarah hi , i bought a present for your win " " thank you " and he went without saying a word, she didn't mind at all as she already lost interest in him.

Sarah went outside and saw John still standing there beside a new car which was rapped yo in a Saturn ribbon he smiled at her and said surprise with a happy smile , the expression she never saw and it was the expression she always saw when he was around Rose , and it was quite shocking for her to see that expression

"why the long space of silence asked John? "

" um it's nothing i was just mesmerized by your gift , that's all

" let's have a ride " " you mean right now ?

" Yeah right now

um all right let me take my purse cuz i gotta buy some things for the party I'm going to hold on a party tomorrow evening

" ugh ! really ? am I invited,

yeah of course she smiled at him bluntly ,

John kept quiet on their way to the shop , realizing that he hurt her really bad

"Leah have you got the listing details correct" ,

yes dad !

, Dad i .... Well very good then, tomorrow we will be going to Los Angeles,. .

what! what are you saying dad ? I have to attend Sarah's party ,

yes well isn't she coming to Los Angeles as well you can ask her to hold the party there well end of discussion , your mom and I will come late at night , so go fast to bed and pack all the important stuff you want .

" yeah right , how the hell i can pack i think i better call Sarah and talk details "

"miss Leah but don't you want to pack important things ,

oh i almost forgot Leah smiled sideways , at said Mr Thompson , in a pleasing way ..

." Oh alright Leah i understand you want meto pack it for you ,

oh thank you so much , I'll write it down all the stuff you have to pack ..

It nearly took half an hour and she went outside took her car , and called Sarah ,

"hey Sarah were are you at i want to to see you ,

"oh I'm in the shopping mall ,

oh alright I will come quick bas possible

It did took an hour for Leah to get to the mall , on the way when she parked her car , she saw someone standing at the corner of the post lamp Kissing each other hugging each other very tight She smiled down the road thinking man couples are extraordinary they don't really care whose around them do they ,

she locked her car and started walking but when she got closer it was, Rose and Kevin , her hurt struck with a sword and it eventually broke into million pieces , the store she had to reach was exactly opposite to her

her phone rang , she picked up but her voice sounded really bad , Sarah came rushing down the 2nd floor to the ground to see wether she was still there and finally she saw Leah standing like she was about to faint .

"Leah oh dear what happened are you alright ?

She couldn't say a word as she saw John beside her ,

she tried to say ..i ..i saw ..and tears came out of her eyeballs ,

Sarah was shocked to see her cry , she asked her again what happened? What happened?

...she just pointed to their opposite direction were the 3 of them saw Kevin and Rose Kissing and hugging together and he Swift her on her legs to and carried her all the way to the car and carried her all the way to car and let himself inside the car and they disappeared in thin air .

V

REALIZATION OF LOVE

" John whispered Rose ? No ..nooooo he shouted as he shouted loud Sarah started crying really bad so did Leah and John fainted as he couldn't control shock just like last year when he heard that Sam and Rose were dating each other but knowing Kevin and Rose together was the hell he underwent right now,

it was because they both tried really hard to pursue Rose but he couldn't he was thinking that i didn't give her what she wanted i was just there when she needed me but i was not there like forever and moreover Kevin was the only one who rushed to see her in Los Angeles and took care of her , who am I to interfere with her life when i didn't make the move ,

John , John wake up , John ! .shouted Sarah ,she was terrified of seeing John like this it only made her remember about Rose...

"Ugh! ... Sarah , i .. he cried tears rolled from his eyes thinking that she was always with him and loved as the way he is , and to know that he loved Rose now he understood how hard it was for her to watch that and shrug it till the end and never showed her true feelings to him that how she got hurt real bad but always puts on a smile ,

" sarah he said very silently still crying and he kissed her holding her her face with his one hand and said I love you, i now realize how hard it must have been for you to see me as a jerk , I'm really sorry I'm really sorry,he cried as soon as Sarah heard those words from him she was puzzled but then she broke out and cried hugging him .

Leah was resting in Sarah's bedroom , she woke up and sat in the bed recalling all the memories as she was blank and was wondering why she was in Sarah's room, but the memory she re - called made her cry again , as she was crying her mom came in the middle ,

"oh Leah honey I didn't know ,

"mom ! Please stop I'm over it ,

let's go to Los Angeles,

I'm ready for the trip let's go

"No Leah you will stay here and manage your business and you don't have to pressure yourself honey ,

college is tuff but don't let the fun away You will never know how things will change and you might even love this new change , we'll see you soon said her father and they left

Leah carried herself out if the bed and when she walked to go out from the room she saw Sarah and John holding hands tight coming to see her ,

oh Leah your awake how are you ? asked Sarah so desperate as she was worrying about her so much

"yeah I'm fine just worried that's all ,

so John how are you doing ? you nearly fainted ,

" John blushed um yeah. that's a sort of thing for me i can't handle shock but thanks for asking ,

so mistress of beauty are you really doing well?

for a moment Leah was blacked out and she started laughing so hard that her tummy hurt

What did you call me ?

she asked John as she was still laughing,

"um mistress of beauty! "

"Why is that ? "

Um well ,

you look pretty that's why

"Oh so what about me ? asked Sarah

"You are prettier to my eye's always and forever "Aww, that's so sweet of you , but you gotta try harder than that and she winked at John "

"Oh wow guess I have to take love lessons instead of music lessons and they all laughed together "

"hey Leah don't you worry about anything as long as we're here , you'll be alright

"yeah i guess I will , since i have John the fuzzy bear she laughed at him "

"fuzzy bear ?

even Sarah laughed hearing that name fuzzy bear ,

i think we should call John fuzzy bear ,

what do you say Leah ?

,yup we should sure do , "oh great, then the 3 of them headed to a greenary land to get some fresh air to release all the tension and pressure they had inside .

As the cool wind Breeze passed by , John looked at Sarah and smiled at her very lovingly that it made her blush and she smiled back blushing so hard , he laughed at her and said man you are so shy women "say Sarah are you going to Los Angeles? asked Leah earnestly but she was looking up when she asked the question to Sarah ,

John was also staring at Sarah when Leah popped out that question

I'm not going"

"What ! said John really yay , ughh ..i mean why Sarah laughed haha .

Look at you, you little baby"

"what ! i don't wanna loose you okay ,

I'm not going to make the same mistake twice I'm going to put my eyes all over you , Sarah. blushed and said what do you mean by that, John looked at her and said i meant what i said he placed his head gently on the grass ,

Leah got up and said i will go home , i have some work she smiled at them and waved but Sarah tried to stop her ,

"It's okay Sarah i just need some time to get thinda out my mind and let's start our company plans tomorrow since your not leaving she smiled at her and she went back to her car and she drove

"Ugh was she cold towards me now?

"Yes she was !"

"well don't worry let's work together , I'll start constructing a new building for you in your name Sarah paused for a moment and John was shocked to see tears in her eyes

"What happened Sarah why are you crying?"

"No it's just that you always do things for Rose without a second guess so when you say something you are doing it for me it means a lot to me that's why

"Oh Sarah i ..i'm really sorry ..i ..i am a jerk "no your not a jerk , i know John i still know that everytime you see Rose i know that look on your face when you see her , and i don't blame you for that ,i know she's your soulmate and that you care for her but i know that one day your gonna realise something and i know that I'm going to see that look on your face looking at me exactly the way you look at Rose , i know things will turn around someday and that you will love me for me i know that

"Ms Leah are you alright you seem kind of in a temper mood ,

"Ms Leah just promise me that you won't loose yourself ,

Leah stood as she was walking to her room

Mr Thompson i never did find myself then how wioll i loose myself ?

"Mr Thompson realized something terrible and he decided to follow Leah wherever she goes ".

"Kevin , umm ..aah ! you promised not to do it today... aaah..

"I'm sorry I just can't help fucking you all day long "aaah ... Ugh ..Rose breathed really high and she Hugged him tight as she couldn't control anymore and he took the whole intiative ,she was sticking on the wall and finally he brought her to the bed Spreaded her legs and fucked her fast this time she shouted really loud

" aaaa..h ..Kevin..aah .. he loved it he loved every minute of it whenever she moaned his name he was tempted in high spirits that made him to fuck her even hard,

he came up to her breasts and started licking all the way down to her vagina and she moaned real hard and Kevin couldn't stop doing it because hearing her voice and saying his name was the most treasured memory he wanted to have

he then kissed her everywhere and turned to her back side and he started licking her all up she closed her eyes in embarrassment and he started fucking her ..aaah moaned

Kevin and the sound of him made her happy and content he shouted her name and they were both moaning the whole night .

"Rose couldn't wake up as her body was paining really bad Kevin carried her all the way the bath and this time he didn't try to fuck her as he was tired as well so they both cleaned themselves but still to him she looked really hot ,

she was walking to the side of the bed to get some night dress and as she wore

"Damn she looks so hot ,

Kevin pulled her backwards, and kissed her in the neck passionately and she kissed him back on his lips and they both went to sleep as they were still tired

VI

KEVIN I LOV E YOU

Rose was swirling on the bed and she climbed on Kevin's body and laid her head on him "hey good afternoon sweetheart wake up let's go somewhere out, but Rose didn't want to go anywhere so she just lifted her head up and saw Kevin and then she slept on him he teased her by pressing her ass, wake up, she screamed and starred at him blushing, he laughed at her

"Okay let's wash our face and go have lunch "make me some said Rose looking at Kevin like a baby he smiled at her and said okay baby whatever you say

"Rose washed her face and went to the wardrobe to wear something nice,she wore a frock with Rose pattern and the color of the frock was half white and she was looking very lovely

"Kevin was staring at her and he said you look really beautiful either way "what do you mean by either way exactly?" "Um well, I love all of you, your boobs your belly button,

your...." okay okay stop said Rose as her face blushed really hard I get it. Kevin smiled at her and said you're very shy but I love it the most now let's eat shall we?

yes we shall said Rose and they started eating their lunch which was really tasty, to Kevin Rose looked like a little bunny chewing carrots Rose looked at Kevin when he pinched her cheeks politely she smiled back at him and fed him back they even took a photo together eating together and sleeping together as the couple's do

"Say Rose we should go somewhere don't you think? "Were?"

"Well France, Switzerland some places and create memories before we get married so after marriage we can do it differently I just want to live while we're young and not to mention when we have sex in different places it will be more interesting than you know

"Rose smiled back at him and said you are so interested in sex! "Nope I'm interested only in you and he hugged her tight and kissed her on her neck "Rose couldn't control her moaning she sounded loud it turned on Kevin

"Oooh looks like someone is enjoying, Rose blushed and she bite him back on his neck, he carried her to the kitchen slab and lifted her frock up and removed her panties and her removed his trousers, and started fucking her hard . and he removed her whole frock so did he

"Rose said Kevin let's do it in the bed not here he looked at her and said no let's do it here We will do it in the bed soon but i want to do it here now

Rose couldn't stop him as she liked it too so she thought of letting him take control After 2hrs she was in the bed sleeping beside Kevin she thought this man is a real sex machine but she smiled at him and brushed his hair with her fingers and kissed his cheek saying I love u Kevin, I love you too sweetheart .

VII

SARAH LOVE ME TENDER

Sarah, hi said John, she was still in her pajamas she blushed furiously seeing John

I will be back in 2 min she rushed to her room washed her face and wore pants and a prep top and Jacket She combed her hair and wore coral color lipstick which she loved and used the most and now she looked really good after dressing up "Oh looks like i have to go to the shop and buy some lipsticks "

"Really ! what kind? asked John coming to her room Aaaa! John when did you, how did you, who did ..! ..she was blushing furiously but his facial reaction made her blush, even more,

He came close to Sarah and pinned her on the wall his one hand on the wall and the other on her hips pulling her close to him, he saw how beautiful she looked that he never noticed and he kissed her passionately but he didn't stop his hand went down her pants but Sarah pushed him and said maybe not now

"What do you mean not now? he got mad "Sarah told my sisters will hear us "Oh! that's right " "then let's go to my place" "What about your mom?

"Nobody's home they went to a fair and they will be home by evening " he grabbed her hand and took her to his home which was just beside her home

"John carried her when they entered his home, the maid saw John and Sarah but didn't interrupt them " " he threw Sarah on his bed and he removed his clothes his body was very seducing for her to get her eyes off "

"John, are you forcing yourself to do this or do you want to do it because you love me? he saw her and said you wouldn't be in my bedroom if i didn't love you and i don't do anything by force it only makes things worse and yeah you're right but i want to have a first time with you if that's ok?

"It's alright as long as you don't change your mind and love me forever "

"yes i will love you forever" "now let's start "

"The moaning sound was high and they were in good spirits John started licking her vagina and made her scream loudly the maids in his house blushed and they wore ear muffs so that they won't hear those sex screams

" he then started kissing her whole body and started fucking again and from the back he also did sideways his one hand on her vagina fingering her, his other hand touching her whole body and fucking her at the same time in a sitting position John enjoyed everything about it

especially her moaning sounds and they did that for the whole morning and they were sound asleep,

John woke up first he pulled the bed sheet slowly without waking Sarah and she was covered with another bed sheet he spread on her before they slept he cleaned it himself and he went out and asked one of his maids for sanitary pads and they gave him, they blushed while they gave it to him, he smiled bluntly and said thanks and he went back to his room

he went to the shop saw her panties size and bought 2 whole boxes and sanitary pads, he then remembered the lipstick she was talking about the early morning in her home, so he bought a bundle of lipstick with make-up sets he bought her lots of dresses and he smiled cunningly and asked the shopkeeper to pack those bras and lace panties, sexual fun dress

"The shop keeper women blushed, Master Kevin is buying from our shop and that is too full of girl stuff, "the other salesperson said not to mention it's sexual fun too they laughed at him "Pack this for me "Oh yes sir

" he must love his women so deeply..aww

"Kevin was so happy to hear that, he went to his room Sarah was still sleeping he then gently pulled her to him it was seducing as she was naked but he didn't want her to scream after she woke up seeing herself naked

so he carefully wore her new dress he changed her pads just clear her vagina with water slowly since he didn't want to wake her up

"After an hour Sarah saw she was sleeping on someone's lap she woke up and saw it was John "Hey honey woke up already " "Sarah blushed and asked him did we ? "yes we did i even changed your clothes and changed your pad " "Sarah blushed at him" "I am your husband baby "

"you're taking all the credits mmph

"John laughed you're like a little hamster "

so look i bought you lipsticks and also the lipsticks from my mom's company and makeup set to make sure it matches your skin type "Sarah's eyes were full of hearts she climbed onto John's lap and kissed him saying thank you he blushed seeing her cute smiley face.

"Sam the project is been going really well said his best mate Patrick

Thanks, bud he smiled back at them and his business was going really good

"Hmm, I guess Rose would have joined with Kevin right now,

i think i need to make sure that I'll call her

"Tring Tring, ugh it's Sam "Tring Tring,

ugh, it's Sam Hey Sam!

Oh hey Rose how are you doing? Rose didn't speak much she just wanted to be straight she thought of telling him on the phone but she stopped and just casually chatted with him on the phone as she knew it would be rude to ask him to come home and to spend time with her so she just discussed how Los Angeles was and it was not like she was never there and she didn't want to go there as well so she just went with the flow

"Leah was ordering everyone in her company to make a seat available for Sarah as she was going to work with Leah but not beside just like the rest of the members in the company

"Miss Leah, we have arranged a seat for Sarah " Good I'll call her but Sarah didn't pick up "John it's Leah, she is calling me "Oh great just like i thought "What do you mean?

"I mean she is using you, well to put it in apt words she is taking revenge on everyone who pissed her off "What do you mean pissed her off !? Sarah nearly shouted in agony

"Sarah she wanted to be Kevin's girlfriend but she was getting nowhere with it so after those conflicts she had you as a friend that is you were not in a relationship, so once she found out about it, that is you and i got together she felt pissed off so she wants to make you suffer and then let you off nice and easy but she also doesn't wants you to know that it was her

"what!"

VIII

I CANT DO THIS IM SORRY

"Ugh she sounded fine but somehow i think there was someone with her thought Sam as he ended up the call

"who was it?

"oh it's Sam

"What did he say?

"Oh just work stuff

"Mmm, you didn't tell him?

"No, i thought of telling him in person

"Mm good choice

"Secretary get me details about Rose

"yes sir "

"she might have, no that's impossible, she wouldn't but oh never mind, i just want her to be happy that's all

"Leah had. scornful look glaring at her phone

she thought of addressing Sarah directly she couldn't control her temper anymore she went straight to her home she started to throw things in her home all the maidservants were shocked to see her like this,

Mr. Thompson was in the backyard, one of the maidservants informed him that Ms. Leah came inside and started throwing things please sir only you could calm her down

"Leah! Leah dear come here, she saw Mr. Thompson and ran to him and she hopped on him as he was tall it was alright to hold her without falling he hugged her tight and said it's alright, it's an alright sweetheart she cried in his chest so much he took her to the room laid her down and brushed her head

"Leah my dearest rest for a while, we will go out in the evening okay don't worry about anything

it was 5 in the evening Leah woke up and recalled everything and she remembered that Mr. Thompson told her that he would take her out somewhere so she dressed and came out of her room she saw that Mr. Thompson was having a basket of chocolate and in the other bag full of beach clothes

Leah looked guessing

"Mr. Thompson, are we going to the beach?

"Not exactly I'll tell you when we get there and maid Marisa is coming too

"okay no problem

"Sir we have found the results about Ms. Rose

okay good you may leave

when Sam opened the file he dropped it

as he saw the picture of Rose and Kevin kissing in a diamond shop

No ! he shouted

he then arranged a plane ticket to New York

and this time he was not about to leave New York without making things right

No! he shouted he just didn't want this to happen and he will do anything to make her come back to him no matter what the circumstance is

"Kevin told Rose that he should probably go to the company to handle things

"alright

"but what will you do alone?

"who said i will be alone

Were you going?

"To John's

Okay be careful

Sure

" Rose took her bicycle she thought the car is a big headache if it's a cycle it will be very nice

she also thought of buying chocolates on the way she was so happy to go to John's home

She reached there as quickly as possible, and she knocked on the door John opened the door and was shocked to see Rose and he was also drunk

he got drunk because he regretted why he even had sex with Sarah when he didn't love her for real, he saw Rose as if she was naked, and he could help it he just carried her to his room

Rose thought he was just playing with her like they used to play before but when she saw he went to his bedroom she had a bad feeling

He gently placed Rose on the bed and came close to Rose he asked her do you still love me?

" what?

"I love you but i am in a relationship with Kevin

" I don't care and that's not gonna last

I know you decided out of guilt, you deeply love Sam but you forced yourself, and let me guess you probably even had sex with him am i right?

" H .how could you tell !?

"Rosy i know you better than anyone

But since you gave a chance for Kevin

Um well .. it's alright but if you don't want to i can totally understand but just be careful alright

I have no idea how are you going to control Sam as John was going on Rose popped out a question that startled him

"Do you want to have sex with me?

I ..what are you talking about Rose !?

"i don't want to be responded to in anger

"Okay then well let's eat chocolate

but John came close to her and said

Yes I really want to but it's just that I'm your friend and I'm just your friend

"Do you want to be my boyfriend?

"Actually your husband

"but we all know that it won't happen

"It can?

"How ! he asked in. great shock.

You have to convince everyone it's simple as that

as Rose was doing the talking

John stared at her thighs

as he was sitting beside her in the bed he touched her thighs and started removing Rose blushed so badly and said John what are you doing?

he didn't let her speak he kissed her, he removed her dress he started kissing her breasts and squeezing them she mourned her voice made him so horny that now he started licking her breasts and he came down licked her belly kissed her belly, and came down to her vagina and he was licking it for 20 min that she mourned so bad that his maidservants heard her scream, she shouted John ...aaah ..

stop it ...aaah. She was blushing so bad

"You're enjoying this

"No .. i ...mm ..aaah

"I love you Rose I'm in love with you i want you to be my wife and mine alone and my only

after an hour Rose was sleeping soundly on John's bed from what he experienced with Sarah was very different with Rose when he did it with Rose it was very different it was like he never wanted to stop fucking her, she made his mood so high that he was so happy and so horny he smiled at her and brushed her hair

Sarah was standing in John's room and saw everything John noticed her but he was not about to get shocked or say sorry he just said I'm sorry Sarah but it's not the same with Rose she is my lifeline and she will always be

I'm sorry I can't do this anymore, i love her

as he was saying he saw Sam beside her

He saw John said nothing he just said take care of her, don't let her go, don't let her to Kevin i don't trust him at all but j trust you

Common Sarah let's go

Sam grabbed Sarah's hand and took her to his car her rode to a nearby lake and saw Sarah was really sad, he carried her she blushed to say Sam what are you doing?

"I just don't like to see my little puppy worry

"Puppy ! so what are you?

"I'm your dad

There was silence between them and he started to laugh, Sarah said, hey Sam stop laughing

he carried her and said common puppy bowwow

She started laughing as he carried her and goofing off at the same time

Wow said Leah as she watched through the horizon her smile was really big,

Mr. Thompson was so glad that he brought her to the beach to experience joy like she never did as a random person,

for the first time in her life, she saw all kinds of people she ran to the beach as she was a little kid even miss Marisa was so happy to look at Leah enjoying so much, they finally realized that she is just little kid with a lot's of love in her heart and yet a beautiful innocent soul, what a lovely girl

"Mr. Thompson, Ms. Marisa ! come and join me this is awesome she waved her hand her smile was priceless

"Leah give me a pose

"She smiled at them

"Mr. Thompson asked someone on the beach to take a picture of them and a priceless picture together with Mr. Thompson and Ms. Marisa

Yay! this is the best oooooh she shouted as time passed by it was 5 PM in the evening they went home on the way Leah said thank you so much, Mr. Thompson, i feel alright now i think we should come here sometime

"Yes dearest

"Ms. Marisa thank you for coming said Leah

"as she went inside every maidservant surprised her wishing her Happy Birthday miss Leah

She was so happy that she started crying in happiness, everyone hugged her and said we love you miss Leah and when we started walking inside ..she saw her parents

"Happy birthday honey

"Mom, dad i thought you guys

"yes yes that's a big story

we were on our way but then i remembered it was your birthday so we hurried to home, when we came home we heard from our maidservants that you went outside so we thought of surprising

you, Leah, were so glad that she had someone who cared after all this time she wanted only one person to love her but she almost forgot that she had loved and is being loved continuously

Leah shouted i love you so much you guy's so much.

"John said Rose staring at him

"Hey don't stare at me like that, i can't help it

Oh and one more thing Sam came and talked to me he knew the whole thing and he was okay with it, he just told me that it was alright as long as it was not Kevin

"what

"I want to see him

"yes first have a bath. and then we can depart

"Okay

" Rose hurried downstairs and saw John waiting for her by the car

"you ready for this Rose?

"of course I'm ready

"Okay then let's go

Sam was with Sarah on a game shop playing together

"Sarah I'm gonna beat you. Oooo

"No way I'm gonna win. Yeaaaah

as they turned Sam officially won and when Sarah turned to see Sam she fell on his chest she blushed that instant so did Sam,he held her and said, careful missy

Um ... sorry, so. before she could say a word the phone rang in Sam's pocket he took the phone and saw that it was John

"Hey what's up man

"Hey, Sam where are you?

"I'm at the gaming center, why what's wrong?

"Stay there I'm meeting you

"Sure

"Who was it, Sam?

"It's John Sarah paused for a moment and said okay let's buy him something to eat before he arrives

"sure thing

"After an hour John's car came in

"John came out of the car and he held Rose's hand

Sam didn't see clearly who it was but when he went near it was Rose he shook his head and saw her

Rose jumped on him hugging him tight said that she missed him so much and she started crying

Sam cried seeing Rose cry, John was shocked to see that Sam cried for her so did Sarah, John then knew it was time for him to move on as he saw how truly they loved each other and it was very wrong of him that he took advantage of her

He just told to Rose

"Rose hold on to him tight just like this for the rest of your life, i don't think anyone will understand more than Sam does enjoy you too

come on Sarah let's go home

"Sarah refused she said no i want to play

I want to spend time with all of you today now

alright said John

"you guy's coming ?

"sure said Sam

Then they started playing they had so much fun that they forgot it was past 10PM in the night

They danced and had lots of fun

On their way home Rose slept on Sam's lap like a little puppy Sam cuddled her and held her tight

John saw how much Sam cared about Rose that they look perfect with each other, even though John or Kevin competed with Sam.

It was always Sam and Rose in the end even sex couldn't break their relationship that was very fascinating for him in its own way

They finally reached home and Sam carried Rose placed her in a bed kissed her on the cheek and said Good night and he went to his home

Sarah and John wished their Goodnights and went to sleep

"The next morning Rose woke up and pinged Sam

"Hey Rosy said, Sam

"Sam we need to go to college

"Are you sure?

"what do you mean by sure !?

"of course, we are going

"Besides I'm not going to let go of my dream to become a pop star

"alright alright pop star let's make your dream real

"yup we sure are

"John John wake up Rose is waiting for you in the hall said his mom

"what! aren't we supposed to take a leave, we landed here like 6 hours ago

"yes yes now go and have some fun, wake up

"John woke up in trance and picked himself up and went to the bathroom freshened up and he wore leather pants and a t-shirt colored red and a vest black he even took sunglasses and a bunch of lollipops, his mother asked oh! look at your new fashion sense ..awww sweety even the maids in his house blushed

"John saw Rose and Sam together, Rose started to talk, John stuffed the lollipop in Rose's mouth and do not be rude but please stop talking until we get there Sam your driving and I'm sleeping

Rose didn't mind she already knew that John gets clumsy when he doesn't have good sleep so it was not a problem for her at all she started chewing the lollipop

as soon as they got to college the whole campus was crowded

Rose got off the car and saw why it was crowded, one of Rose's fans came and told her hey Rose it's really glad to see you

, we are having a competition here, it's the 3 rounds competition

"Rose asked so we have to get selected at the first round am i right?

"Yes and not just that nobody actually wins the first round is judged by the Rock band themself

but this time things have heated up this time the judges are from the singing leads and guess what i think not even the Rock band can win this

Rose didn't actually care about what she said she just wanted to win this,

after all, it was her childhood dream not like the ice cream she wanted like yesterday

, Rose was furious but Sam hugged her and said it's alright we are with you

Josh came out of nowhere and said wow hold the phone aren't you Kevin's girlfriend why is Sam the basketball captain hugging you ..ohh you like to play with boy's ugh you little pipsqueak let me see how you will win this 1st round as he was going on about Rose Sam punched him in his face when he saw Rose crying

"That's enough, she is my wife and if i hear any shit from anyone I'll make sure that they will never play music at all

and he carried Rose to the car and a hand stopped him it was Sarah

"wait Sam the 1st round is about to commence

"No look at her she is crying there is just no way

"I can, we will sing All of me

"Are you sure

"yes

" John said ... I'm gonna beat the crap out of him

"Since when did you come, where did you go? asked Sam

"I can, we will sing All of me

"Are you sure

"yes

" John said ... I'm gonna beat the crap out of him

"Since when did you come, where did you go? asked Sam

"Dude i went to wash my face, i can't walk like a zombie all over the campus

"Rose started laughing wiping off her tears

It maRose started laughing Sarah, John, and Sam were happy to see that

"That settles it we are singing zombie

"wait you're going to dress me as a zombie

Everyone laughed and said ...no u big goof we are going to sing that song

"Ohhhh i see alright

They headed for the numbers and they were 15th

they did practice and this time Sarah joined them as Kevin was not available and the 3 of them except Rose didn't like the idea of him joining their band

as time went by their opportunity came and they started to sing,

everyone was startled and drowned in Rose's voice,

Sarah's way of drumming and Sam was the lead singer and the side guitarist

John was looking amazing when he played the music keyboard even the Judges couldn't say no to their

performance and the song zombie wasn't just a song it was a song that makes

everyone or anyone sings together in joy

The whole campus got lit and everyone was happy and dancing together it looked like a concert on the outside

"while Sarah's mom was cruising through her campus she saw Sarah how extraordinary she looked while playing the drums even Maggie was spellbound

no one actually ever knew that she could play musical instruments

Sarah personally learned music lessons when she was in middle school,

Daniel her cousin challenged her to a piano competition so she learned every instrument and won over Daniel but asked her to promise him not to tell about that she won over him

as the crowd went wild ..the judges confirmed to give the results in 2 days

"What ! 2 day's ! shouted Rose

"Sam laughed and said wow cool up Rosy

We can practice something else or make a youtube video

"Then youtube video is

" What now?

The music studio Sam built for Rose was filled with members now and it looked more beautiful than before,

they practiced the song "clarity"

and Rose's voice was melting in the music

Sam, John, and Sarah were concentrating on her more it was more like she was standing on a stage and the light was on her she shined so brightly when she sings

"Okay um guy let's take some Break

"you still sleepy asked Rose smiling at him

for a moment John was staring at her bluntly and didn't say anything he came close to her it definitely made Sam and Sarah mad but he went down his pockets and stuffed a lollipop on her face again

"stay cute doll face

" What ! said Rose taking her lollipop out of her mouth

"I just need some sleep, so toodles

"Damn he's got some nerve said Sarah

"Yeah, I'm gonna rip it off if he doesn't come clean tomorrow said Sam staring at John who lead himself out of the room

so what now? said Rose as she looked at Sarah and Sam

"Well let's take a short break and upload our music video said Sam

"that sounds great honey said Rose and she blushed and thought oops. Ugh i mean

"Oooo ..can you say that again asked Sam teasing her, she blushed even hard and said

No .oo hey stop it. he pulled her close and kissed her Sarah took a pic of them while kissing and send it to both of them and she teases them saying hey check your phone adorable couples

Sam and Rose checked their phone Rose said Sarah .. she blushed furiously, Sam said good job partner to Sarah and smiled at Rose.

Rose was searching for a copy of Daniel's album and finally she fou, the first hit song

she was sulking into his voice and she remembered last summer how crazy he went thinking about Daniel so she decided to dress up and go to the pop star stuff-buying store she dressed herself up, she thought of pinging John, but she remembered he didn't have a good sleep so she went by herself and she bought all the new stuff and new albums of Daniel's and she saw someone discussing a youtube channel called Shining star

Ugh i think I heard that name before, hold the phone it's my youtube channel

"Hey look it's Rose , oh my gosh it's you

Oh ! can i have Your autograph

um sure

as she left the store she went straight to the ice cream shop and there was a huge crowd

she didn't mind she just pushed herself inside to buy her favorite ice cream and

she saw Daniel he saw Rose and pulled her close to him and admitted that

"Okay okay, you guy's just want to know if i have a girlfriend or not right?

"Yeaaaah shouted the crowd

He kissed Rose and said she is my girlfriend the famous singer on YouTube

Rose said what!

IX

LOS ANGELES &KEVIN

As Sam gets finishes his shower and sees the news and get's frustrated, he then calls Rose and asks her what is going in, she tells him that she just went to buy ice cream and saw a huge mob and saw Daniel

"Okay stay out of his sight, where you at I'll come and pick you

"exactly at 5 min, Rose got in the car and she was really disturbed and Sam kept his hand on her thighs saying

"Hey, it's alright okay I'm right beside you.

"Rose's eyes were teary she tried to smile but she couldn't.

"Sam parked his car in a nearby green field a private one and he carried her there

"he said I'm always with you, I love you

I will never let go of you and I know you love me so deeply too.

"Rose cuddled him back and said yes I love you so much, Sam

Rose, will you marry me?

Rose said yes without thinking

"Let's get engaged said Sam smiling at her

" John tried to reach Rose but she didn't pick up as she was busy with Sam on the green field

Only after an hour did Rose get home and sees John's missed calls, she thought of calling him back but she knew that would ruin the whole surprise

She called Sam and said when shall we keep our engagement?

"Tomorrow said Sam and kissed her on the phone

Rose only thought was she had to get ready

" Leah was thrilled to meet new people she even planned to Hawaii the coming weekend with Mr. Thompson and Ms. Marisa

"Dad I would like to know myself and enjoy myself a bit before getting serious with the business work and stuff like that

"I understand honey

"so Leah went to the parlor for a change

"Ugh Rose ! she thought seeing her in a parlor was a shock

"Hey said Rose looking at Leah

"Hi " she replied with enthusiasm

"Rose said you are finally free

"Leah was speechless to know that Rose could actually see through her

(Leah's thoughts)

"Now I see why these guys hang around with this woman it's because she soothes their souls

wow it's really good to have a friend like that

and Sam .. wait didn't Kevin the one who kissed her

(Reality)

" Rose so why you came to a parlor"?

" Oh Leah could you keep it a secret

I and Sam are getting engaged tomorrow and you're invited

"Leah was speechless again, then what about Kevin !?

"Rose said um Leah I don't love Kevin

I love Sam I deeply love him and don't worry Kevin is all yours

"Leah said but he ain't paying attention to me

"he will don't worry

"Hey Sam called John through the phone, so what's all the fuss about my mom and dad talking about something, I just want to know what's it about.

"just wear a tux and come to my home this evening

"ugh!

"The evening arrived

"John saw Rose and Sam together standing next to them, he was first confused

"Sarah, what's going on?

"Ugh, you don't know?

"No, of course not!

They are getting engaged

"What he said very slow

after the engagement party, it was just friends meeting

"so this is why you didn't pick up my call asked John to Rose

"I'm really sorry John, I just want to surprise you

"well you really did, anyways congratulations

he got up and brought a drink for Rose and Sam

"Cheers to you guy's said John smiling at them

"Now it was clear to him that no more Rose but only as a friend so now his only concern should be on Sarah

As he was sinking into deep thoughts he had a phone call

"Hey John congratulations you guys are going Viral on YouTube

"What !?

(8)"Yes and not only that your band is invited to Los Angeles to perform on the stage

"Hey, the guy we are gonna Rock.

"Were? asked Rose.

It looks like our YouTube channel git really hit and they want us to perform on the stage in Los Angeles

Rose nearly jumped upon hearing the news

Yayyyy

"Leah packed all her stuff and checked twice she even bought a manga book she used to read when she was young and she bought a lot

Even Mr. Thompson was mesmerized by how she changed but the real reason behind it was actually Kevin

"Okay lot of creams makeup, manga book then oh yes chocolates yes very important

(Flashback)

I love Sam i deeply love him and don't worry Kevin is all yours

"Leah said but he ain't paying attention to me

"he will don't worry

(Reality)

" Ugh I was finally happy and now he is single again, but luck me 'cause this time Rose is engaged to Sam, I guess I will just trust the timing

Okay Mr. Thompson let's giddy up yahoo

(10)As she wanted to be in the midst of everyone Leah took her private flight because she was always careful about traveling and she wanted traveling to be fun and cozy, after 2 days of traveling she finally reached there and her eyes were sparkling like stars in the sky she was so happy that her happy hear couldn't handle it

She then went to her Room unpacked her bag took a towel and went to the shower to freshen herself up and took a nice deep sleep as it was evening

She knew that she should rest and she was happy that she was with Mr. Thompson for the first time and in along a distance trip

"yes. I'm lucky...

The next morning Leah headed straight to the beach wearing her favorite beach outfit she ordered it from her dad's company and also a unique one, while she was passing there was a bunch of boys who saw her

"Man look at that hot stuff, Kevin was just sitting beside those boy's even he turned to see who it was and he was shocked to see Leah he got up and went straight to her and said

"Leah !?

Leah turned around and was shocked to death seeing Kevin, she was spellbound

"Kevin took his towel which he was wearing around his neck and covered her breasts with putting his towel her neck and grabbed her hand and took her to the end side of the beach where no one would follow them

Leah just followed without saying a word, she still thought was she dreaming? is this real? if it's a dream let it continue

Hey guy we are here said the team in Los Angeles as they came out from the flight

Rose was really exhausted she climbed onto Sam and he carried her all the way to the hotel they laid their stuff and got freshened up

Sarah and Rose are in a room so John and Sam

They had dinner and went past asleep as it was 10 PM in the night

"Sarah woke up in the middle and thought of how she is gonna perform in a huge crowd made her nerves chill so she took a dress robe and she heads to the balcony, she saw someone was already standing there watching the stars

"The next morning Leah headed straight to the beach wearing her favorite beach outfit she ordered it from her dad's company and also a unique one, while she was passing there was a bunch of boys who saw her

"Man look at that hot stuff, Kevin was just sitting beside those boy's even he turned to see who it was and he was shocked to see Leah he got up and went straight to her and said

"Leah !?

Leah turned around and was shocked to death seeing Kevin, she was spellbound

"Kevin took his towel which he was wearing around his neck and covered her breasts with putting his towel her neck and grabbed her hand and took her to the end side of the beach where no one would follow them

Leah just followed without saying a word, she still thought was she dreaming? is this real? if it's a dream let it continue

"Hey guy we are here said the team in Los Angeles as they came out from the flight

Rose was really exhausted she climbed onto Sam and he carried her all the way to the hotel they laid their stuff and got freshened up

Sarah and Rose are in a room so John and Sam

They had dinner and went past asleep as it was 10 PM in the night

"Sarah woke up in the middle and thought of how she is gonna perform in a huge crowd made her nerves chill so she took a dress robe and she heads to the balcony, she saw someone was already standing there watching the stars

Kevin finally talked to Leah and said, are you aware that you have a cleavage that makes any guy nuts then why are you showing it off in front of everyone he scolded her holding her arms tight

"Then what about you, can I show it in front of you?

"..... Kevin let her go and said, I'm a bit depressed right now even if I have sex with you I don't think I will be happy about it cuz I was at my happiest when I had sex with Rose I love her

Yea I know you love her .. said Leah, but she is engaged to Sam

I know that, look Leah find someone to fool around I'm not interested to do anything I want a piece, and don't show off your body like that

"Leah said, it's my wish since you are not interested in me then I might actually find a guy who is interested in me for me

Kevin really didn't mind what she said he was just frustrated thinking about Rose

He got up and took a swim in the ocean to take his mind off things as he was diving he was lost in his thoughts thinking about Rose and hearing her screaming sex voices which made him even cry more

"Hey it's gonna be okay said Sam to Rose and they started their performance and everyone loved it

It was a huge crowd of people awwing and waving hands, they were going crazy they never realized that and

Rose was amazing everyone went crazy about her

as the program ended everyone the backstage

Appreciated Rose and the rest of her band

when Rose was very happy John, Sarah, and Sam weren't as they saw Daniel on the who offered her a chance to be a world-famous pop star and she agreed to it

In other words, they don't have the right to tell her no, so they decided to tell Rose that they are going to cheer her up silently but she has to live her dream without them at least for a while

As they discuss things Rose stays in Los Angeles with her Father and performs songs while Sarah, John, and Sam get back to New York

ABOUT THE AUTRHOR

JANNET RF

Jannet Rf has her bachelor's in Information technology and is talented in writing novels and short stories, her first was published at the age of 11 and she writing since then, and she is famous for her fiction story.

The first book Summer loves the one I cherish.

her dream is to become a successful author and blow the minds of readers and continue her journey of writing more novels and short stories

Works Of The Author

WORKS OF THE AUTHOR

BOOK #1- Rs- 150

BOOK #2 - Rs - 200

SHORT STORIES - Rs - 334

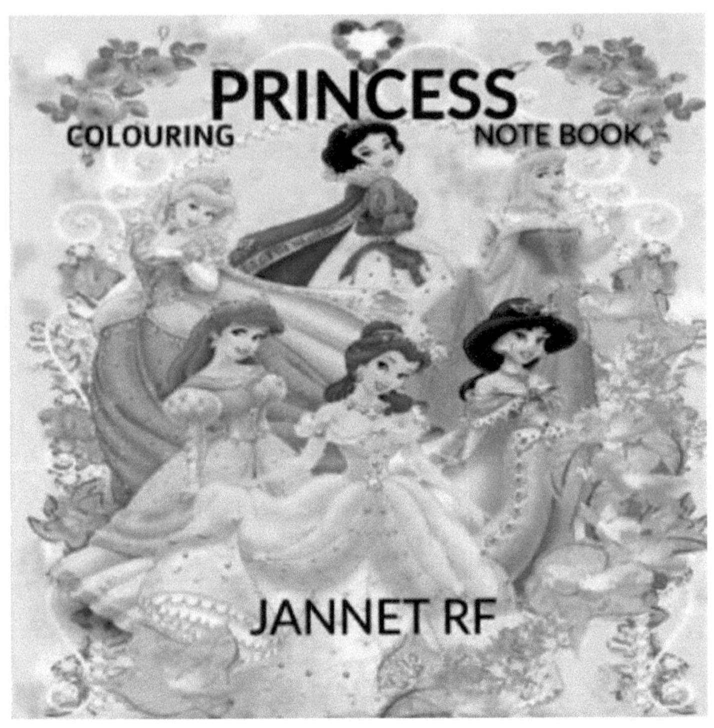

PRINCESS COLOURING BOOK Rs - 1,005

FLORAL ART - Rs - 423

SAINT ANTHONY OF PADUA - 130

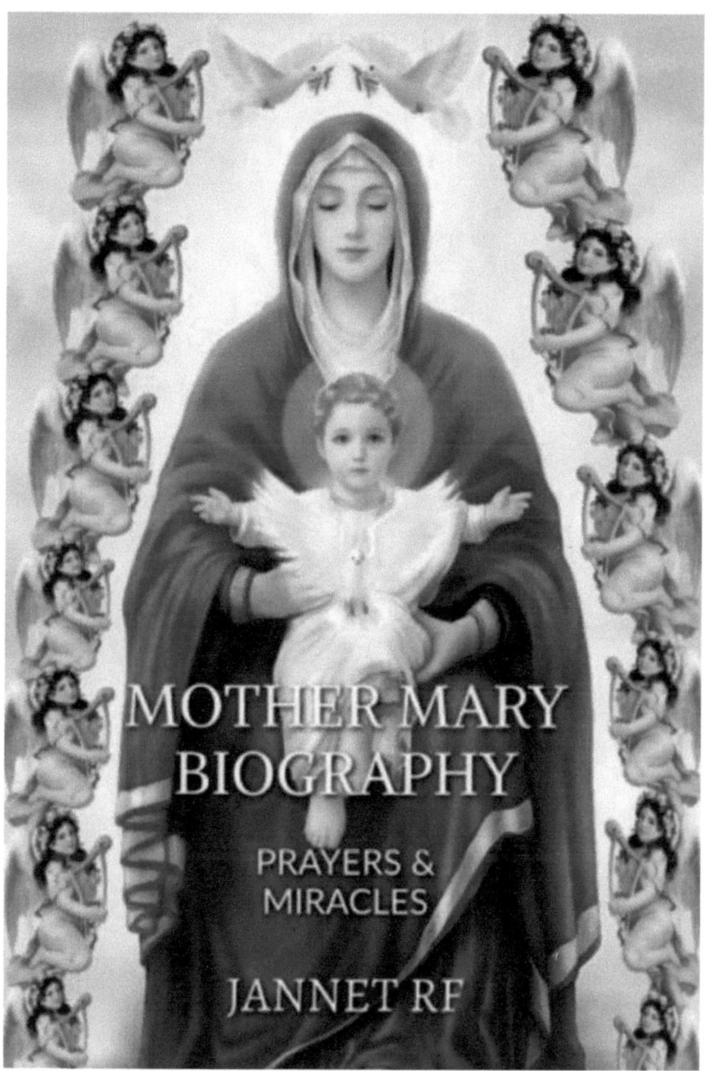

MOTHER MARTY BIOGRAPHY - 200

Printed by Libri Plureos GmbH in Hamburg, Germany